Flying High, Pogo!

by
Constance M. Foland

American Girl®

Published by Pleasant Company Publications
Text Copyright © 2002 by Constance M. Foland
Cover Illustration Copyright © 2002 by Allen Brewer

Author Acknowledgments:
My first thanks goes to Peter Citrolo for being the best gym teacher ever.
Many thanks go to Barbara Seuling and the Thursday writing group. I would
also like to thank my dearest Meggan, for loving Pogo so much. And to my
Michael, thank you for listening.

Visit our Web site at **americangirl.com**

Printed in the United States of America.
First Edition
02 03 04 05 06 07 RRD 10 9 8 7 6 5 4 3 2 1

A catalog record for this book is available from the Library of Congress.

ISBN 1-58485-535-5 (pbk.)   ISBN 1-58485-624-6 (hc)

For Mom

Dear Diary,

Woohoo!!! Have I got news for you! I'm going to gymnastics camp for a whole week. Only two fifth-grade girls got picked to go and I'm one of them. I can't wait to tell Mom!!!

Jumping for Joy!!

Pogo

Dear Diary,

I should have known it wasn't a good idea to ask Mom about the gymnastics camp when she was at work. I was helping her at Kids' Kraft, the shop she owns, when I told her. At first she hugged me and told me how proud she was. That lasted for about three seconds. Then she got into the money thing. Even after I told her that the school will pay for half if we pay for the rest, she made a face. She started going on and on about bills and how slow business has been ever since our competition—the newer, bigger paint-it-yourself pottery shop—opened downtown. I told her I had to find a way to go to camp, that I can't waste my potential. I told her I'd ask Dad for the $300, and she said, "Talk about wasted potential."

I really wish my parents would get along better. They've been divorced for two years, but they still fight, and Mom says mean things about Dad all the time.

She's mad at him because she had to give up her "free spirit" life to go back to work. I'm a little mad at him, too, for going off and starting a new family. But that sure won't stop me from asking, or even begging him, for something I really want.

Keeping my fingers crossed,

Dear Diary,

Remember that other fifth-grade girl I said was going to gymnastics camp, too? I didn't really want to stink up my diary pages talking about her, but now I have to get it out.

Victoria, who I secretly call "Icky Vicky," sashayed into the gym this afternoon bragging that her mother took her shopping and got her all-new camp stuff! Already! She even brought one of her outfits to the gym to show off. Of course, everybody was oohing and ahhing over some stupid pink neon jog top and matching shorts.

When she noticed I wasn't paying attention, she strutted over to me and said, "Did you get anything new yet?"

I said, "No," and kept on stretching, like I didn't even care.

So then Victoria looked me up and down and said, "Well, you don't want to wear old stuff, do you?"

So I said, "Old clothes are comfortable. I like them better."

Victoria just smiled and said, "Yeah, I used to think that, too . . . when I was in elementary school." Then she jogged away on her tippy toes, in perfect gymnast style.

I almost yelled out, "Victoria got her new clothes at Kmart, everybody!" But Victoria was already gone, chalking-up by the bars, and I knew she wouldn't hear me.

Steaming,

Dear Diary,

Today was my day to spend time with Dad. We went for a walk in the park. Then Dad took me out for pizza. It would have been fun, I guess, except he brought his baby, Grace. He usually leaves her at home with Rachel, my "so-called" stepmother, but sometimes Rachel works weekends at her new job.

Grace is eleven months old, and Dad carries her around in one of those pouch things. She slept for most of the morning, which was just fine with me. Then, when I tried to tell Dad about the gymnastics camp and ask him for some money, Grace opened her mouth like she was trying to talk. Since she's only a baby, it came out as a little gurgling sound.

Dad looked down and said, "Oh Marshmallow, Honey, what?"

I felt sick. I just cannot believe that Dad calls this smelly little ball of dough Marshmallow. I thought I was the only one he nicknamed, when he changed "Patricia" into "Pogo." But I guess everything is different now since she came along.

I wasn't going to let her get to me, though. After all, I was here first.

"Dad, you know that camp I want to go to this summer?"

"Yeah, it sounds wonderful." He kept fussing

over Grace and didn't even look up at me.

"I'm sure it is. But the thing is, Dad, it costs $300."

Finally I had his attention. "Oh, really? That's pretty expensive."

"I know, but it will be so worth it. Do you think that if Mom pays half, you could pay the other half?"

"Oh, Pogo, I wish I could. But now that I'm a stay-at-home father, money is pretty tight on my end. Especially with a new baby in the house." Then he smiled at me like that was the end of the story.

He actually had the nerve to ask me if I wanted to go to his apartment and help him with Grace. He was mad when I told him I wanted to be paid for it. He said, "Pogo, she's your sister, for heaven's sake."

I almost said, "She's only my half sister, remember, Dad?" but I didn't want to push my luck. Grace was already fussing and crying, and Dad was working up a sweat trying to calm her down.

I sort of felt sorry for him when he dropped me off. Grace was wailing so hard that Mom actually came over to the car and asked him if he needed help. Of course he faked a smile at her, then roared off into the sunset. I guess I know who took care of me when I was a baby.

Wishing I was an only child, *Pogo*

Dear Diary,

I'm sitting outside. My mom just passed by and asked if I was sulking. I told her I'm reflecting. That's the school counselor's term for writing my feelings down. She gave me a notebook when my parents first got divorced and told me to say whatever I wanted in it. She told me I needed a container for all my anger.

Well, didn't my parents expect me to have some less-than-pretty feelings about this whole thing? One day my dad was hugging me good-bye, telling me I'd always be his round-off, back-flip baby, and the next day I was in school taking a spelling test like every other Friday of my third-grade life. Did they just expect me to swallow that like a Happy Meal with extra fries?

I told Mom I'm not sulking, but she doesn't believe me.

Why should I sulk? Just because my dad said he couldn't afford a measly $300 for camp and gymnastics is only THE most important thing in my life? Why should I be mad? Just because he quit his job so he could stay home and take care of his new baby and spend every cent he has on her? Why should that bother me??

Mom grumped when I told her that, and she said

his support money is barely enough to keep me in food. She also said she's sorry she doesn't have more money herself and she'll do her absolute best to figure something out. In the meantime I'm sitting on the sidewalk waiting for my best friend, Iris. She's coming over to help me think of ways to make money. She's really smart, and she always has good ideas. Plus she understands how much gymnastics means to me, even though SOME people don't have a clue!!!

Not sulking,

Pogo

Dear Diary,

It took Iris and me all afternoon to come up with ways to get money. Here's our list.

Ways to earn $$$$$:

1. Yard sale—This would be OK except I already gave away all of my old clothes and toys. And Iris never gets rid of anything. So between the two of us, there's nothing to sell.

2. Pet movies—This was really Iris's idea. She got a video camera from her grandmother and she's getting good with it. She said I could make the pets look pretty and then she'd film them. We'd comb them and put bows in their hair and stuff, then charge for the tapes. One problem: I'm afraid of big dogs. Small ones, too. So I guess that's out.

3. Collect cans, bottles, and newspapers—I came up with this idea. But Iris said, "What about the Can Man? My grandma says he's really poor. We can't take away any of his junk." She's right, so I let that one go.

4. Mother's helper—Iris and I really like this idea, except we can't think of anyone around here who might need us. It's too bad, too, 'cause we both like little kids. I help them at my mom's shop so they don't glop paint all over their pottery projects. Mom says I'm good with little kids, too. She says she

would give me money for helping her if she could just get more people to sign up for parties at her store.

5. Artwork—If you can call it that. Iris wants to paint rocks and sell them. I said, "Iris, that's just plain goofy. If people want painted rocks, all they have to do is collect some from their driveway and decorate them. Jeez!" Iris kept quiet till she came up with her next idea, which was:

6. Odd jobs—When Iris said "Odd jobs," I said, "Like what? We're too small to mow lawns, there aren't any leaves to rake, and it's not like we know how to fix broken stuff." So Iris said, "I'm just trying to help. Maybe if you would stop doing cartwheels and flips all over the place, you could come up with something more useful." I told her I think better when I'm upside down or flying through the air. And that's exactly when it hit me.

7. GYMNASTICS SHOW!!! We both agreed, it's perfect. The kids at school are always asking me to do flips, wanting me to show them how I bend myself into a pretzel, and daring me to walk on my hands all the way down the hall. So why not put on a real show and charge them for it? We'll have it in my backyard and sell tickets. I just know everybody will come.

Bouncingly yours, *Pogo*

Dear Diary,

I made up some flyers for the gymnastics show. They look really cool, 'cause I got Iris to take some pictures of me doing handstands and splits. I did the writing part, and then we cut and pasted the whole thing together.

Mom let me copy them myself, at her store. I copied a few other things, too, like my hands and some quarters and a few paper clips. I was about to copy my teeth smiling when Mom walked into the office.

She said, "What are you, nuts? Don't you know that thing could blind you?"

I told her I had my eyes closed, but she kept nagging.

"I was just about to compliment you for being so industrious, too, working so hard to make money for camp. But now I see you're in here fooling around with expensive machinery."

I wanted to say, "It's a copy machine, Mom, not a Porsche." But I thought that might make her madder. She's so testy lately about money, she yells over the teeniest things.

I quickly held up the stack of flyers I had made.

She looked like she might snap and say that I made too many. But then the door chime rang and a customer walked in.

Saved by the bell,

Dear Diary,

Dad called and invited me out to dinner tonight. I was about to say no, but then I breathed in a smell like hot cat food frying and saw Mom cooking. So I quickly said, "Hey sure, I'd love to go. Let me just make sure it's OK with Mom."

Wouldn't you know it, he brought Grace. When he came to the door, he was wearing her in one of those sling things. I said, "Is that kid attached to you or what?"

And he said, "Oh, it's so wonderful having a baby."

I glared at him and said, "Huh. I bet you didn't carry me around in one of those."

Dad smiled and said, "It's all so different now. Fathers do these things for babies."

I wanted to say, "Yeah, fathers do things with OLDER daughters, too, you know." But I didn't.

Mostly it was because Grace had started whimpering. As soon as she let out a peep, Dad moved in on her. He unstrapped her from the sling and laid her on the grass. "Whatsamatter, Gracie?" Then he started making all these hand motions in front of her face. I looked at him like he was psycho, but he didn't even notice me. He started tapping his fingers together and saying, "More? More?"

I said, "Dad, what are you doing?"

He said, "I'm trying to teach Grace sign language."

So I said, "Dad, she isn't deaf."

He said, "It's a new thing. Babies can learn to talk to you through signing."

I made my own sign for crazy nut.

But Dad kept going. He motioned to Grace like he was holding a cup and drinking. Then he started squeezing his fingers together and pulling them up and down, saying, "Milk? Milk?"

Meanwhile, I'm thinking to myself, *What is she, a dairy farmer? How's she supposed to get that that's a sign for milk?* I don't know what Grace thought, but she sure didn't stop crying.

Finally, Dad picked her up and started rocking her and cooing in her ear. "Whatsamatter, Sweetums? Hungee belly? More moo-moo?"

Hearing this, I was about to barf, so I said, "I gotta hit the bathroom, Dad. I'll be out in a minute."

By the time I got back, Grace had stopped the bawling and Dad was ready to go.

Had enough of moo-moo,

Pogo

Dear Diary,

I got Mom to watch me do my routine today. I called her outside only when I felt really ready. Then I asked her to give me some tips. It's not like she knows a whole lot about gymnastics—she doesn't. But she *is* a good dancer, so she knows what looks graceful. The only problem is, she's a hard judge. Today, after I did a body wave followed by a *tour jeté*, she smiled and shook her head.

Like the true professional I am, I went right on with the routine and finished without even looking at her. Then, after my ending, I walked over to where she was standing and said, "What? What was so bad about it?"

So she said to me, "I'm not trying to be mean. You told me to be honest. You want it to be perfect, that's what you said."

She's right, as usual, so I asked her what I needed to do to make it better. She helped me make the body wave less stiff. She said, "After all, you're a wave. You're water. You have to flow." Then she told me to put more life into the *tour jeté*. "Move like you're a bird, not a propeller."

She must have been in a good mood today 'cause she even helped me pick out music and showed me some old dance steps she used to do. She played all these oldies for me, and I finally found a song called "Rockin' Robin." It's really bouncy and quick, perfect for my routine.

Flying like a bird,

Pogo

Dear Diary,

I helped Mom out at the shop today and she actually paid me for it. That wasn't her plan, of course. It was kind of a bribe, the way she ended up giving it to me. I was doing handstands against the wall and using one of the benches in the shop as a balance beam. And she got mad at me.

I said, "Mom, gymnastics is in my blood. I need to do this."

She said, "You're going to need crutches if you keep jumping around like that. Now quit it."

I kept going, though. Just a couple cartwheels and a split here and there. Nothing big. But Mom lasered her eyes at me and pointed to the sign she has hanging over her cash register. It says, "You break it, you bought it."

I really think Mom is just too no-nonsense lately, so I said, "Mom, lighten up, take it easy." But Mom was serious, and now I'm benched. She told me to sit at one of the tables where people paint and to stay there. Then she gave me some stuff to touch up and said she'd pay me five dollars if I'd sit still and finish everything before closing time. So I sat and filled in where some little kids couldn't finish. I painted the laces on a two-foot sneaker. Then I fixed up a giant crocodile. Do you have any idea how hard it is to paint a hundred crocodile teeth?

Trying to sit still,

Pogo

Dear Diary,

Iris and I tacked up the flyers all over school today. The show is only a week away! We wanted to sell tickets in class, but the principal said we couldn't. She says it's against the rules for us to make money in school. Iris thinks we shouldn't sell tickets on the playground either, but I said, "Don't worry. That's outside. The principal never told us that was against the rules, now did she?"

Iris complained and said that her grandma would kill her if she got into any trouble, but I finally convinced her to go along with me. We made eight dollars (tickets are two dollars apiece), and five kids promised to bring in money Monday. This might be easier than I thought.

Getting rich,

Dear Diary,

Saturdays are the best—Open Rec Day! Only a few kids were at the gym. I was so happy 'cause that meant I could work on any piece of equipment without waiting in line much.

I was about to start my work on the uneven bars when Miss La-Di-Da, Victoria, strolled in. She stood right near the bars, smiling. I should have known something was up when she gave me a big cheery hello.

I did a great mount, a kip/squat on, then swung myself up to the high bar. I hated that Victoria was watching. Bars are definitely the hardest of all in gymnastics for me. And easy for her. I tried to act like she wasn't there.

I did a few back hip circles to get warmed up. I wanted to work on my giant swings today, but not with her watching. So I went up into a handstand instead. That's when I noticed that my palms were starting to sweat. Plus they were getting sore. I had rubbed a lot of chalk on my hands earlier, but still they felt like they were starting to rip.

I swear, it seemed like Victoria was staring at me through binoculars. I couldn't take any more and I started to rush. Just as I started my dismount, I slipped and fell on my butt.

I expected to hear her cracking up, but she didn't. And that might have been better. I could have laughed, too, and made it seem like I was just fooling around.

Instead she walked over to the crash mat where I was recovering and said, "Hey, did you get your letter from camp yet?"

So I said, "No. What letter?"

Victoria said, "I got one today. It tells you what to bring and stuff. Plus they tell you when you need to send in your money."

I jumped up off the mat. "When? When do we need the money?"

"In a few weeks, I think. My parents already sent mine in."

Of course. Knowing her, they probably own the camp.

"Oh . . . well, that's cool. My mom will probably write a check for me this weekend, then." I shook my hair, making like it was no big deal. "See you around."

"Don't you want to know anything else about camp?"

I wanted to hear everything about camp, but I definitely couldn't stand to hear anything right then. Especially not from her. "No thanks," I told Victoria. "I'll wait till I get my letter."

Just call me an Open Wreck, *Pogo*

Later . . . Before bed

Dear Diary,

I checked through the mail as soon as I got home from the gym, but I didn't find any letter from camp. Maybe Victoria is playing games with me?

Wondering,

Pogo

Dear Diary,

Dad called this morning and begged me to help him take care of Grace. I said, "Dad, aren't you forgetting something?" I waited for him to fill in the blank.

"I know, Honey. I know I told you we'd go skating today, but Rachel got called in to work."

I said, "Dad! You promised."

Grace started crying in the background, and Dad made cooing noises to her like I wasn't even on the line. I swear, I almost hung up in his ear. Then I said, "I'll only come over to help if you pay me ten dollars." Dad agreed in no time.

It didn't take a genius to figure out why. Grace was crying her eyes out with no sign of stopping when I got to his apartment. Dad says she's cutting a new tooth and she had kept him awake all night.

Right after I got there, Dad passed Grace to me like he was handing off a football and escaped out the front door. He said he was just running to the laundry room and he'd be right back.

Holding Grace while she screamed in my ear was not exactly what I had in mind when I agreed to this. I had to do something to quiet her down before I lost my marbles. I made monkey faces at her, but that made the crying worse. Then I sat in

Dad's old rickety rocking chair and sang her some songs. My mom says I have a pretty voice but I think I squeak like a kindergartner playing the violin. However it sounded to Grace, she sure didn't stop wailing.

Finally I switched on the radio and tuned in some loud disco music. I was actually doing it to drown out the sound of the crying, but the music didn't help. So I started dancing while I held Grace. At first I just swayed from side to side. Then I started moving, doing spins and really rocking. I even got Grace to do some baby gymnastics. I held her with her two little legs straddled around me, then gently tipped her backward and slowly flipped her over, holding onto her arms. She stopped crying!! After a little while, she even started to laugh.

"Hey! You like this!" I wasn't sure if the baby books my dad reads would say it's OK, but I held Grace upside down by her ankles. Grace reached out toward the ground, so I lowered her until she could touch. Then I wheelbarrowed her across the rug, her hands taking tiny steps. She laughed at that, too, so I picked her up under the arms and swung her around in a circle. Then I remembered something Dad used to do to me. I threw Grace up in the air. Big smile. She loved it, just like I did.

I threw her again. Big, big eyes. I held her way up above me.

"What do you think, Grace? You gonna be a gymnast?" She giggled, so I flipped her once more.

When Dad came back, he yelled, "What's with the radio?" But then I showed him Grace's smiling face and he got the picture.

I should have charged him fifteen dollars for doing such a good job.

Baby-sitter extraordinaire, *Pogo*

Dear Diary,

Wow!!! I must have practiced my routine a hundred times this morning. I got to school early. The P.E. teacher usually opens the gym for the girls on the team, so that we can work out. Iris came to help run the music for me and did some videotaping.

I think the pressure of the show is getting to me 'cause I kept goofing up in one spot or another. Like when I worked on my round-off back handspring, back tuck. I flew into the mount, running as fast as I could, got lots of height on the handspring, then flipped into the tuck. Every time, I just about nailed it, but then I took a step and almost fell forward at the end.

When I got too exhausted from doing that over and over, I practiced the dance section of the routine. It's new 'cause I added a few really cool steps from a dance Mom taught me. It's called *jive*.

When I was ready to tape again, I said, "Iris, come on, let's do it."

She nodded from behind the camera.

While the music played and the rockin' robins whistled, I did some high bouncy knee kicks. Then I spun around and launched into a skip-hop step. At the end I made something up. I swiveled on my toes and wiggled my butt a little. Iris started cracking up.

I stopped dancing and said, "That's a new move! It's called the Pogo!"

Iris walked up to me and pointed her video camera right in my face. "Ladies and gentlemen, we have Pogo Winston here, world-famous gymnast. Miss Pogo, can you give us a few words about the preparations for your upcoming show?"

So I said, "Miss Pogo can't talk to her adoring fans—right now she's got work to do!"

But Iris kept going with the newscaster bit. "Miss Pogo, can you please tell us what it's like to do your routine so many times in one day? Don't you get dizzy with all that flipping?"

"Iris, the show's this Saturday!" Then I walked away from her and got back into starting position.

She put the camera down and raced over to me. "I'm sorry. Are you mad? Don't be mad. I'm just trying to have fun. Please? Don't be mad at me."

I took a deep breath and said, "Iris, I'm not mad. Just stop playing around, OK?"

Iris nodded, and I started my routine again. This time I pounded through it without stopping.

Shooting for perfection, *Pogo*

Dear Diary,

I've gotten into trouble before, but I never thought it would be so bad. This morning, Vick the Ick herself, Victoria, showed up at the gym, too. I had just finished having a little talk with myself about perfecting the back tuck when I heard her behind me.

"What are you doing here, Iris?"

Iris mumbled something I couldn't hear.

So then the Ick said, "Well, I mean, you're certainly not a gymnast. Are you sure you know how to film the right moves?"

Iris looked down, and some of the other girls started to snicker.

Once she had an audience, Victoria kept it up. "I mean, don't you need daintier fingers to work the camera?"

Iris still didn't do anything. She didn't even look at Victoria.

So I walked over. I said, "Leave her alone. She knows exactly what she's doing."

"As if you could tell."

Next thing I knew, we were screaming into each other's face. I don't even remember what I said. All I know is that when I looked up, the P.E. teacher was standing over me. And Victoria and I both got reported for fighting.

Iris offered to go with me to the principal, to tell what really happened, but the P.E. teacher told her to go to class.

So now I'm sitting in after-school detention, just for sticking up for my friend. I'm so mad I want to bite somebody.

I was supposed to call my mom and tell her, but I pretended like I was staying late for gymnastics. I am *so* in for it if I get caught.

Reflecting from jail,

Dear Diary,

Tonight Iris called me up, crying.

I said, "Eye, what's wrong?"

She said in this big sobby voice, "Why do kids always pick on me? Why? Am I that goofy?"

"No, you're just . . . unusual. Victoria's a jerk."

"What do you mean, unusual?"

"I mean it in a good way, Eye. Not bad. You're unusual like an artist is."

"Kids call me a four-eyed freak. They laugh at my clothes. I can't help it if my grandma makes me wear sailor dresses and Boo-Boo Kitty T-shirts."

They laugh at her pink ruffly socks and high-water pants, too, but I didn't think it would be helpful to point that out to Iris just then. Instead I took a deep breath, 'cause I knew I had to say something big. "Iris, listen. I have to tell you something and I don't think you're going to like it."

Iris blew her nose. It sounded like a trumpet blasting on the other end of the phone.

"Kids pick on you 'cause you let them. You never stick up for yourself."

"Is that a reason to tease somebody?"

"No, it's not. But they know you're easy to bug. They know you won't fight back."

"I can't fight back. I don't even want to fight back. My grandma would kill me if I fought back."

"I don't mean you should punch somebody out. I just mean you should tell them off once in a while. Use your words to get rid of them."

"Use my words? What am I supposed to say when they call me Bubble Butt? Do I really have a fat behind?"

I swear I only paused for one split second. If you wanted to write it, you wouldn't even put a comma where I hesitated. But Iris jumped all over me.

"You think I have a bubble butt! You would have answered no right away! You think I'm fat!!!"

Before I could say anything, Iris hung up. I started counting to ten 'cause that's how long it usually takes her to call back.

By the time I got to eight, the phone rang.

"I didn't mean to hang up. Sorry about that. I hope you're not mad. You don't really think I'm fat, do you? My grandma says I'm just 'large for my age group.' That's all it is, isn't it?"

Iris is very large for her age group. She'd be large if she were in eighth grade. But I didn't say that. I just said, "Iris, don't worry. Really. You look fine." Then I quickly changed the subject so I could get Iris onto something else.

Trying to keep the peace, *Pogo*

Wednesday, May 29 . . . Surrounded by pennies
. . . When that letter comes, I'll be ready!

Dear Diary,

Mom handed me her big juice jar full of pennies
and told me I could have them if I counted them
and wrapped them up! So now I'm sitting on my
bed, which is covered with pennies, making piles of
ten, then turning them into piles of fifty, which is
how many you need for a roll.

I asked Mom to help me, but she said she needed
some "alone time." I'd like to spy on her just once
when she has this alone time. She disappears into her
room like it's a holy sanctuary and I don't hear a peep
for about an hour. I tried to follow her in one day,
but she just made these sad droopy eyes at me and
said, "I know you'll understand about this."

I guess that's her nice way of saying, "Stay out of
my hair for a while."

I don't mind. I have a big job to do anyway.

Swimming in a sea of pennies,

Pogo

Dear Diary,

Did you know that 1,700 pennies make seventeen dollars? That comes out to thirty-four rolls of fifty cents each. It took me most of the night to wrap up the pennies. When I was done, I made some noise outside Mom's door to see if she would stir. She told me to come in. She was just waking up from a nap. She kissed me on the forehead and thanked me for not disturbing her. She promised me she'd cash in the pennies tomorrow.

Rolling in dough,

Pogo

Dear Diary,

Iris and I spent the last two days going door-to-door in the neighborhood selling tickets to the show. It was hard, not like selling cookies or candy. When you walk around selling sweets, people take one look at the beautiful catalog pictures and go, "Ooh, I'll take one of those and two of those. My husband just loves coconut."

Not with tickets to a gymnastics show. Oh, no. Everybody on the block wanted to see me do a trick first, like I'm a circus dog. So I spent the afternoon doing back flips and aerial cartwheels. One old lady wanted to see if I could put my foot behind my head (as if that had anything to do with gymnastics!). And after I did it, she didn't even buy a ticket.

When we stepped off her porch and the old lady couldn't hear me, I said to Iris, "You watch. I'll toilet paper her house so bad on Mischief Night, she won't be able to open her front door."

But Iris wasn't paying attention. She was kneeling down, aiming her camera at the dirt.

I said, "Eye, what are you doing? We still have ten more houses to go."

But she kept filming. So I squatted down next to her while she followed the path of an ant carrying a crumb.

I said, "Iris, do you really think filming a bug is more important than selling tickets to a show that's only a couple days away?"

Without even looking up she said, "Maybe to me it is."

I let out a sigh that could have filled a hot-air balloon, and stood up. "OK. Fine then. If that's your decision." Then I stormed off.

Pretty soon Iris caught up with me. "It's not more important than the show. It's just more interesting."

I gave her a look and said, "Are you with me or not?"

Then Iris said, "I guess I can do both."

Everything smoothed out after that. Iris stopped only a few times, and we managed to sell fifteen tickets before the sun went down.

Getting richer,

Pogo

Dear Diary,

Mom's been in a really bad mood lately. Today was the worst. When she got home from work, I could see she had been crying, and she started yelling and cursing because people have been calling her for money she owes.

I felt bad 'cause I hardly ever see Mom cry. Yell? Yes. Curse? Sometimes when she's really, really mad. But cry? Not my mom.

I got scared a little, too, 'cause Mom kept talking about how we don't have any money. I don't know what she means by that, exactly. Like how bad it really is. I'm kind of afraid to find out.

OK, I'll admit it. I'm a little selfish, too. Mom's crying got me worried and made me think, "Goodbye gymnastics camp." I haven't bugged her about camp at all. I'm afraid to even bring it up.

Mom went to her room to be alone for a while and that helped calm her down. I wish I could help her get her mind off her problems. But how can I, when I'm one of those problems?

Trying to stay out of Mom's way,

Saturday, June 1 . . . Showtime

Dear Diary,

Iris and I gathered up all the chairs we could find, and arranged them in the yard for people to sit on. I thought seats would make it seem more like a real show.

Iris brought some balloons and she went off to hang them in weird places and film them. I have to say, I don't get it at all when Iris is making her videos, but usually when she shows me the tapes afterward, they look really cool.

When I went inside, Mom had a surprise for me. She made me close my eyes. Then she brought out my pink leotard and turned it around to the front. Shiny sequins dotted the whole neckline, and more sprayed out into a sunburst along the side. Then she told me to sit down, and she did my hair in a French braid. She actually made up my face, too, which is a miracle 'cause she usually doesn't even let me wear lip gloss.

The show is happening in a few minutes. I'm waiting inside, trying not to sweat, while Iris gets the kids sitting down and ready to watch.

Preparing for a cool entrance,

Pogo

Dear Diary,

I am never leaving my room again. Ever. I may not even come out from under my desk. Today was supposed to be one of the most exciting days of my life and instead it was the worst. Me and my great ideas. I had the biggest chance to make money for camp, and I blew it.

All the kids and some of the grown-ups in the neighborhood came to my house for the gymnastics performance. I don't even know how many people showed up, but it was a lot.

Iris made this big deal announcing me, and I started out by doing some tricks. First I bounced into a long pass with a round-off and five back handsprings after it. That got everybody going. I did some other little stunts, too, like dive rolls over a cushion, and cartwheels into splits. Then I walked across the yard on my hands. Kids always think that's the greatest.

When I felt ready, I gave Iris a sign. I wasn't nervous, 'cause I had my routine down. I knew every step by heart. Plus once I got started, I knew my audience was into it.

Then suddenly, right in the middle of my routine, a big dog, and I mean he was Clifford-sized, ran into my yard. I froze. Completely froze. I just stood there like an idiot, while the music played on and on, praying that the big mutt would go away. But then he started running in circles around me and he tried to jump up on me. He put his front paws right onto my shoulders. The kids all roared with laughter, but I was shaking right down to my bare toes.

I looked over at Iris, panicked. Luckily she realized I was stuck and she faded the music out and started clapping like a lunatic, making like the show was over—which it definitely was, even though it wasn't. And then I ran into the house.

I locked myself in my room. Of course, my mom followed me right up to my door and tried to get me out. At first she said things like, "You did such a wonderful job. Come out and talk to your friends." When I didn't move, she said, "It's not so bad. We got rid of the dog." When I still didn't answer, her voice got a little edgy and she said, "Don't make me come in there. Do you hear me?"

She's serious, I'm sure, but what can she do? Ground me? She'll have to set my room on fire to get me out of here.

Inside for life, *Pogo*

Dear Diary,

It wasn't Mom's threats that finally got me out of my room. It was the chanting outside my window. After the last time that Mom came to my door and I told her to leave me alone, I heard the kids calling my name ("PO-GO! PO-GO!") louder and louder, till I finally got up and looked out. The kids were all cheering, with Iris leading them on—shy Iris, who won't even stick up for herself! I couldn't stay inside, even though I felt like the biggest idiot on the planet.

I just told myself to "suck it up," like they say in the Olympics, and then I ran back outside. I actually cartwheeled my way across the yard, my arms and legs like the spokes of a wheel spinning nonstop. I made it seem as if I was just waiting for an encore, like a famous ballerina would do.

The kids loved it!! They liked it even more when I let them take turns on the trampoline, and we made the whole day into a big party. I showed some of the little ones how to do swivel hips on the trampoline, 'cause all they knew how to do was jump. Then I taught them how to play Popcorn with two bigger girls on the sides and one teeny kid bouncing in the middle.

Lots of the kindergarten kids were trying to do

cartwheels but they had the wrong approach, so I showed them the right way. I told them, "Arms up and reach out, not down." They actually learned, too!

We took videos of everybody, and Iris says we can have another party and show them later.

After all the kids left, Iris handed me an envelope stuffed with money. $ixty-eight dollars!! I'm waiting till tomorrow to show Mom. Maybe then we can have a real conversation about me going to camp.

Tired but happy,

Pogo

Dear Diary,

I can't sleep. I've been awake for the last two hours trying to come up with ways to make more money. I got so excited about how much I've saved so far that I didn't even think about how I'll get the rest.

When I went into Mom's room and told her I was worried about getting money, she said, "Hey, join the club."

So I said, "Mom, that doesn't really help me."

She said, "Well, can you just try not to worry about it for now and go back to bed?"

I didn't say anything.

"I know how you feel. I swear I do. We'll talk about it in the morning, OK?"

When I was little and I couldn't sleep, she used to invite me to get in bed next to her. Then she'd say, "Think of a happy place. Imagine yourself where you feel safe and warm, and the next time you open your eyes, it will be morning."

I have to say, it was a lot easier to imagine that happy place when I was tucked in next to her, all close and snuggly, with no worries on my mind. I guess those were the old days.

Back in my own bed,

Sunday, June 2 . . . Under the willow tree

Dear Diary,

Right before Dad picked me up this morning, Mom sent me outside to get the mail. (I guess with all the excitement of the show, we both forgot to bring it in.) Usually I don't even look at the letters that come because they're never for me. But ever since Icky Vicky got her letter, I've been hoping, hoping, hoping. Today when I reached in, I finally found an envelope from Camp Springboard. It was addressed to Mom, so I rushed inside, ready to beg her to let me open it. I slid the bills and stuff onto her desk first and held the camp envelope separate.

Mom didn't even look up. She took one letter from her pile and ripped it open. "Another notice from the landlord? What does he want from me now? Blood?" Then she said a few words I don't really want to write in my diary.

Quickly, before she noticed me standing there, I slinked off to my room. I didn't really plan to keep the camp envelope a secret. I just thought I'd wait until an "appropriate" time to show it to her. She would appreciate that, I think.

I also didn't mean to stuff the envelope into my backpack, but I wanted to have it close to me. It felt so important. I didn't want it to get lost somewhere.

So now I'm sitting here with the envelope lying just a few inches from my fingertips, not knowing quite what to do.

Trying not to be sneaky,

Dear Diary,

Here I am back at Dad's. I wonder if he ever thought when he nicknamed me Pogo that I'd be doing this kind of "bouncing" back and forth from Mom to him.

I don't mind so much. When I get bored at Mom's, I get to go to Dad's. And by the time I've had it with Grace and the whole Daddy/baby situation, I'm usually right on schedule to go home. Today, being at Dad's came in very handy.

He was the one who planned brunch, but in usual Dad style, he forgot to buy eggs. So he asked me to stay at his apartment with Grace while he ran to the corner. On his way out he said, "She's a lot of fun these days. She's really getting into things."

I guessed he meant she could do a lot more, but I thought, *That doesn't sound like much fun to me; I came here to spend time with you.*

I wanted to start Grace out on the right foot and not in one of her crying moods, so I smiled at her and tickled her tummy. She made this little motion with her two fingers, wiggling them over her palm, so I said, "Wiggle, wiggle to you, too."

Then she started clicking her thumb and fingers together like a bird beak opening and closing.

I said, "Grace, you look like a silly duck."

She just kept flapping her fingers, so I said, "Sorry, Grace, I don't know what you mean. Come on. I have some important detective work to do."

I put her on the rug where she could play with some toys. Then I sat down next to her and took out the camp envelope. I held it up to the light to try to see inside. I guess that's something that only works on TV, 'cause believe me, all I could make out in there was a folded-up piece of paper. I looked at Grace and said, "What do you think, Grace? Mom wouldn't mind, would she?"

So Grace does the wiggling fingers thing again. I said, "Grace, come on! When are you going to learn to talk? You're driving me crazy."

She must have thought that was funny, 'cause she started to giggle. Then she started whacking the envelope. And before I could do anything, she grabbed it out of my hand and somehow managed to rip it partway open.

I yanked it away from her and said, "Oh, Grace! Look what you did!" Then I thought to myself, *Hmm. Look what she did. I guess I have no choice now. I guess I have to open it up all the way and read it.*

This is what the letter said:

Dear Family of Springboard Camper,

Thank you for applying to our camp.

We would like to make a final list of all

the children attending our second summer session beginning July 22. Please fill out the information below and kindly send us a deposit of $50 so that we can reserve your space. If we do not hear from you by June 15, we will assume that you are withdrawing your application. The balance of the application fee will be due upon your child's arrival on July 22.

There was more, stuff about me getting a physical and asking if I have allergies or any special problems they should know about. (They listed bed-wetting as one of those possible problems—I sure hope I don't get a bed wetter for a roommate. And if I do, she is definitely NOT sleeping in the top bunk.)

But the one line that kept jumping out at me was the one about the deposit. I got into a panic thinking about it. Picturing Mom's face when I showed her the letter. Worrying that she'd scream and say, "Forget about camp."

I was lost inside my mind, thinking about what I should do, when Dad walked in and said, "Reading anything interesting?" For one split second I considered telling him about the camp letter and asking him one more time for some money. Then I looked around at his teeny apartment. I looked at the faded couch that we used to keep in our basement and the scratched coffee table that Dad wrestled into a rented van the night he left. And I thought about how Grace wears my old hand-me-downs, even the really, really used ones. Then I slipped the letter into my backpack and said, "Nah, just some stuff for class."

Trying to stay cool,

Dear Diary,

I think I'm turning into a juvenile delinquent. It seems like every time my mother turns her back, I do something sneaky. I can't even write about it in here in case Mom finds out about my latest trick. As it is, I'm probably on my way to a home for bad girls.

Trouble seems to know my name,

Dear Diary,

I can't stand my mother. You'd think she could pay some attention to me for once, but no. I woke up extra early this morning and I waited and waited for her to get up, but she didn't. Finally, at 10:00 A.M., I knocked on her door and said, "Mom, come on. We have to get to the shop by eleven. And I need to talk to you."

Was she even grateful that I woke her up so she could get to work on time? No. She just groaned like a bulldozer revving up and said, "I haven't even had my coffee yet. We'll talk later."

But, of course, later never came. She rushed to get ready, and then we flew to Kids' Kraft.

That's where I am now. My job today (for zero money!!!) is to clean up the back room. And it's big. She expects me to get rid of all the dried-up paints and any broken pottery pieces, and the worst of it is—I have to clean the bathrooms! I said, "What am I, Mother? Your servant? Do I look like I'm wearing a maid's uniform?"

She said, "Oh, Pogo, you're such a drama queen," and handed me a broom. Then she laughed.

I said, "I don't see what's so funny."

Mom said, "You are," and walked to the front of the store.

I swept up a little bit, but then I quit. I decided to give Mom "a dose of her own medicine," as she would say. If she won't listen to me, then I won't listen to her. When she decides to pay attention to me so that I can talk to her about camp, then maybe I'll help her out. Until then, I'm on strike.

Sitting down on the job,

Dear Diary,

I found the coolest thing to do!!! I made a mini roller rink!!! I was sitting around in back, getting bored, ignoring my mother, when she flung open the swinging doors and said, "Can you come out and watch the shop for a few minutes? I have some business to take care of." Mom didn't even wait for me to answer. She just let go of the door and disappeared into her office.

Out in front, I helped a little kid paint a baseball red (of all colors), and then his friend asked me to help him paint a giant blue hot dog. (No wonder they're friends.) I don't know where their mothers were. Sometimes grown-ups drop their kids off in the store and say to Mom, "Oh, I'm just going to grab a cup of coffee. I'll be right back." And then they whisk out of the store, leaving Mom to baby-sit. Only today it was my turn.

I had already put the finishing touches on the mustard for the hot dog and the mothers still hadn't come back. One little boy was getting whiny and calling for his mommy. I gave him a stuffed bear and tried to get him calmed down. Finally, he sat on the floor and started sucking his thumb and rubbing the bear's nose. His friend, meanwhile, was wandering around the place grabbing at every pottery piece he could reach. Just as I looked up from the thumb sucker, the other kid was yanking a gigantic dinosaur off a shelf.

So I ran over, scooped him up, and said, "Come on, you two. Let's go play a game."

But the thumb sucker didn't move. "We want to skate! Our moms promised us we could go skating after we finish here."

The wanderer grabbed his backpack. "Yeah, we've got our skates! Take us outside!"

He was headed toward the door when I said, "Wait, I have a better place." So I brought them into the back room, moved all the junk and the extra tables to the sides of the room, and made a big open space. Luckily my Rollerblades were in Mom's car, so I ran out and got them.

We loved skating in the back room. The floors are very smooth and easy to roll on. I even rigged up a couple jumps out of old plywood and we skated over those. For such little kids, these guys were daredevils!

"Make another one!" the thumb sucker yelled.

"Yeah, a higher one!" called his friend.

I had to clear out more space, so I started moving a few things, skating back and forth, carrying stuff from one side of the room to the other. And that's when I got my next brilliant idea! Delivery girl!

I could go to one of the shops in town and deliver for them! They could pay me in tips or maybe by the hour. I could make a ton of money that way.

I called out to the kids, "Wait for me here, you guys! I've gotta go tell my mom something." Then I burst through the swinging doors like my butt was on fire.

Setting my wheels in motion,

Dear Diary,

What a terrible way to end the day! Just as I skated out of the back room to tell Mom about my great idea, this big guy came storming out of Mom's office and stomped outside. I knew he wasn't a customer— he was carrying a briefcase and wearing a suit, not exactly how you dress when you want to paint a mug. Mom came out of her office right after him, and just as she did, the two little boys zoomed out through the swinging doors and flew through Kids' Kraft, chasing each other and zipping in and out between the tables.

"What are we running, free baby-sitting in here?" Mom yelled. "This is a shop, not a playground!" A vein in her forehead stood out and her eyes bulged.

It was like the wheels on the boys' skates froze. They stopped in mid-roll. Mom must have known she scared them 'cause she stopped yelling and sat down at one of the tables.

She looked like she was about to cry. I mouthed to her, "What's wrong?" 'cause I knew she wouldn't cry over two kids playing in her shop.

But she shook her head and mouthed, "Never mind."

I snooped around in her office later. I had to find out what had made her so upset. I think I found it.

Her desk was piled high with bills, and the bill on top was marked, with a big red stamp, OVER-DUE—NOW IN COLLECTIONS. I don't know exactly what that means. But I have a bad feeling it $pells out $eriou$ trouble.

Scared to find out,

Dear Diary,

On the way home from the shop, I asked Mom if we could stop and get ice cream. I added, "My treat." Mom can't resist a double scoop of chocolate chip on a sugar cone, and I was trying to cheer her up. (I had already decided to order the cheapest thing for me so that I wouldn't have to spend too much.)

We stopped at Lickity Splits, but Mom insisted on paying. After we picked up our desserts at the take-out window, she said, "What's with you all of a sudden, wanting to spend money? I thought you were saving for camp."

I told her, "I just thought I'd help out a little." Then I tried to bluff. I said, "You know, 'cause of your bill in collections and all." I wasn't really sure what I was talking about, so I said it through a mouthful of ice cream.

Mom shrugged and said, "Hey, we're already buried in bills, so what's another ice cream or two?"

I said, "Is it really that bad?" My voice squeaked out like a hinge that needs oil.

She didn't say anything for a while, just stared out at the stars and the full moon. The only sounds in the car were Mom crunching her cone and me slurping the last of my root beer float. Finally she said,

"Put it this way: I can max out my credit cards totally, or I can close the shop. Closing the shop seems to make more sense." Then she started the car and wheeled out of the parking lot.

I wanted to say, "Then what are we gonna do for money?" but I was too scared to say anything at all.

More than worried,

Pogo

Dear Diary,

I have to tell the truth. I can't hold it in one second longer. I sent in the camp deposit without telling Mom. I know it was a stupid thing to do, but how was I to know we might lose the shop and all our money? I have no idea what to do about this. All I know is that Camp Springboard will be expecting the rest of the money on July 22. And if I don't pay it, I'm scared that I'll get put in collections just like Mom. I'm freakin' out, but I refuse to sit on my butt and do nothing.

First thing this morning I grabbed Iris, to tell her about the delivery girl business, and ask for her help. I didn't tell her about Mom maybe closing the store or the ugly goon with the briefcase. I just said, "Iris, we have to work fast."

And you know what Iris said? "You always have to work fast. Everything with you has to be quick, quick, quick." She snapped her fingers to punctuate the quicks.

So I said, "What's that supposed to mean?"

Iris bent down and tried to pretend she was filming a dewdrop on a blade of grass, but I knew she wasn't 'cause the red light on her camera was off.

I squatted next to her and put my hand over the lens and said, "Iris, what's the matter?"

"I don't think I want to be in the delivery girl business. I fall every time I skate. And my grandma doesn't like me going far away from home."

So I said, "Iris, we need to talk."

Iris just stared.

"Haven't we been friends since kindergarten?"

"Yeah."

"And don't we always help each other?"

"Yeah."

"Remember when your parents got in the car accident and you had to come to my house the first night because the nurses wouldn't let you stay at the hospital?"

"You mean when I couldn't sleep so you read *Charlotte's Web* to me?"

"I read you the whole book, Iris, till you finally wore out your worries."

"I remember."

"Well, this is like that. I really need your help."

Iris sighed. "OK, I guess I can try."

"We'll be really careful, I promise."

Iris turned back to her filming, this time with the red light on.

I knew she wasn't thrilled, but what could I do?

Desperate,

Dear Diary,

Iris and I did a little brainstorming about places that might need delivery people. That's what my teacher says you need to do when you're trying to get ideas. I don't know why she calls it a *brain storm*—I'd rather call it a *brain waterfall* and imagine all my ideas pouring out onto the page.

Here's our list of places that might need two roller-skating delivery girls:

1. The drugstore—Older people always need stuff at the drugstore and they can't always get out to buy it. We could deliver things like aspirin and stomach medicine.

2. The pizza place—We're not too sure about this. Pizza would be hard to deliver on Rollerblades. Not to mention we don't know if we could get it where it's going while it's still hot.

3. Sandwich shop—Maybe. Easier than pizza, but still might need to deliver hot food.

4. Pet shop—Once again, Iris's idea. She can't seem to get it through her head that pets and I are not a winning combination.

I said, "Iris, when was the last time somebody had a real rush on doggie biscuits? And how in the world are we supposed to deliver 20 pounds of kitty litter?"

5. Newsstand—I thought this was a great idea till Iris said, "What do you think the paperboy does?" I guess I'd forgotten about him.

Running out of ideas,

Dear Diary,

Iris and I spent the afternoon handing out coupons and flyers for Daly Drugs. We skated to the store to ask Mr. Daly if he needed a delivery girl (or girls), but he said no. He liked the skate idea, though, and asked us if we wanted to do some other work for him. It was fun, I guess, wheeling up and down the sidewalk giving out coupons to anybody who walked by.

I did most of the work, though, 'cause Iris spent half the time hiding behind phone booths, hoping her grandmother wouldn't see her, and the other half taking water breaks.

Mr. Daly made a deal with us. For every customer who used a coupon, we got to keep the amount of the discount. At the end of the day, Mr. Daly totaled up the coupons: nine dollars and forty-five cents. Then he rounded it up and gave us an even ten.

When we were getting ready to leave, he asked us if we wanted to come back next week. Iris looked at me for the answer, and for a second, I didn't say anything. Finally, I faked a smile and nodded at Mr. Daly. "Yeah, sure. We'll be back."

But I'm not sure at all. Ten dollars used to seem like a lot of money, but at this rate, I'd have to be a delivery girl for fifteen weeks (plus $2) to pay Camp Springboard. That's all through summer and into next school year! And I'm sure that money is small potatoes compared to what my mom must owe in bills. Things do not look good.

Spinning my wheels,

Dear Diary,

On the way home Iris said, "What's the matter? Aren't you happy with ten dollars?"

How am I supposed to feel happy about anything when Mom might not even have a job? I tried to make excuses and change the subject, but Iris didn't go for it. She said, "Come on, I know you. You're never sad like this. If anybody feels bad, it should be me with all the times I fell on my butt today. 'Specially that last one."

Right before we finished, Iris slipped in dog doo. She didn't see the big pile of it on the sidewalk, and it sent her flying. Luckily she didn't land in it. The picture of that made me laugh, though, and pretty soon I told Iris everything.

Iris just listened and didn't say anything for a while. Finally she put her arm around my shoulder and said, "Don't worry. Your mom will figure everything out."

So I said, "Iris, I know you're trying to help, but if my mom could have figured everything out, don't you think she would have by now?"

Iris didn't have anything to say to that.

We made a plan to go back to Mr. Daly's next week. I guess a little money is better than none at all.

Down in the dumps, *Pogo*

Dear Diary,

When I first saw Dad's car pull up this afternoon I got psyched 'cause I thought Dad might have a surprise for me. He used to show up unexpectedly sometimes, with jelly doughnuts or maybe a little toy from the dollar store.

Well . . . before Grace came along he did, anyway.

I ran out to the car to meet him, and there was Grace sitting in her car seat, smiling at me, with jelly smeared all over her face. Dad was keeping up the treat tradition, I guess, just not with me.

"Say hi, Grace." Dad waved his hand in front of her face, but Grace just smiled.

"Hi, Dad. What are you doing here?"

"I stopped by to talk with your mom. But first, how about giving me a round-off back flip, and I'll spot you."

Dad knows I don't need a spotter anymore, but he likes to get behind me and really whip me into the air.

I couldn't resist. "OK."

"Let me just take Grace out of the car and I'll be right there."

Grace, Grace, Grace. That's all I ever hear. It's a wonder he remembers me at all.

Dad put her down on a blanket under the willow

tree. Then he put his finger up to his eye and pointed. "Watch, Gracie, watch!"

He rubbed his hands together and said to me, "Come on. I'm all ready for you."

After I did a couple of tricks with Dad spotting me, I called out to him, "Hey! Just like the old days!" Then Dad tried to do a cartwheel himself. That's when Grace started to laugh. Dad jogged over to her and clapped his hands. "Clap, Gracie. Say yay for Daddy." He held her hands together to show her how. I have to admit, she looked pretty cute when she tried to copy him.

"Still trying to teach her sign language, huh?"

Dad shrugged and said, "Yeah, she'll get it one of these days."

Then Dad picked up Grace and said to me, "I'm going to pop inside and see your mother. I'll be back out in a little bit."

"Why don't you leave Grace with me?" I don't know what made me say that. Maybe I had a feeling Mom and Dad would start fighting, like usual, and Grace's baby ears would have to hear it all.

"Hey, great idea. She can be your cheerleader."

Grace got all wrinkly and sad-looking when Dad walked away, so I said, "Don't cry. Come on, I'll show you some fun stuff."

I put her down on the grass, and she took off in a crawl in Dad's direction. "Grace! Hey! Get back here. Watch this." I did a forward roll. "You want to try?" I grabbed her and put her in my lap. Then I rolled her over.

She giggled. "Come on, let's go backward now." I scooped her up and made her do a flip. "You want to do sailies? Come on, I'll sail you." I stood up and held Grace out in front of me so that she lay face-down across both my arms. Then I floated her back and forth in the air. "Wheeee, Grace. Wheeee!!"

"Eeeeeeee!" Grace chirped. "Eeeeeeee!"

I moved her faster. "Go, Grace, go!"

I don't know if Grace squirmed or I got carried away with the sailing, but all of a sudden I slipped and fell on the grass. Grace landed on top of my chest, then rolled off me.

"Hey! Are you OK?" I prepared myself for a giant wail.

Grace rolled herself over again. Then she lifted her head and smiled at me, showing three tiny baby teeth.

"Grace! You did a perfect landing! Good job."

I hugged her to me, thankful that I didn't do any damage.

Feeling lucky, *Pogo*

Dear Diary,

Things at Mom's shop seem to be getting worse instead of better. Today when I walked in after school, Mom was sitting, staring at a pair of pink pottery ballet slippers. Not painting, not doing anything.

I said, "Mom? Are you OK?" She didn't even answer me. I said, "Hello. Dirt to mom. Come in, Mom."

Without looking up, she said, "The Hewitts canceled their party for Saturday. They decided to take little Tommy and his friends out for pony rides instead. Good-bye, four-hundred bucks."

Not knowing what to say, I grabbed a cloth and started wiping down tables, getting ready, just in case we got a bunch of customers at lunchtime. Or any time. Just so Mom would see that I'm not about to give up.

Pretty soon, she started working, too. But she looked like a zombie, her eyes dark and dull. She moved like a robot as she dusted off the shelves and straightened up supplies. Finally she turned around the "Sorry. We're Closed" sign to make it say "Come In. We're Open."

Open! I wanted to shout!! Come in!! We're open!! But nobody even looked in the window. The only person who stopped by all morning was the mailman. I just prayed he wasn't delivering any bills.

Waiting for the other slipper to drop,

Pogo

Dear Diary,

I was tidying up the paints in the storeroom when Mom stomped into the back and said, "Guess who just called me? Just take a wild stab!!"

Before I could say a word, she hammered back, "Camp Springboard."

Uh-oh, I thought. *Here it comes.*

"They received a certain fifty dollars. All in cash, I might add."

"Mom, let me explain."

"Explain what? How you signed my name and gave yourself permission for a week at camp?"

"That was before—"

"I never once said you could go to camp!"

"You never said I couldn't."

"We can't possibly afford camp! What were you thinking!"

"Mom, I—"

"I, I, I! How selfish can you be?"

"Mom, please—"

Mom took a really deep breath and puffed out her cheeks.

"I can't believe you just took it upon yourself to do this, without even asking me."

"If I asked, you would have said no."

"Well, I might have good reasons for saying no."

"And I had good reasons for wanting to go to camp. One of them is to get away from YOU!"

I didn't wait for Mom's reaction. I just bolted out the door. She called and called to me, but I ran like Maniac Magee down the street, through parking lots, over the churchyard. I ran till my chest burned like ice, and then I sat down on this curb to rest.

Catching my breath,

Pogo

That night . . . In bed

Dear Diary,

I went to Iris's house after I ran away. But Iris wasn't home, and of course, Mom found me there sitting outside. She roared up in front of the house and said, "Get in the car. Now."

I swear, she growled like a black bear coming out of hibernation—not that I've ever heard one, but I can just imagine.

When I got in the car, Mom peeled out and started yelling. I usually complain about wearing my seat belt, but this time I strapped myself in extra tight and held on.

"Who do you think you are, forging my name?"

I tried to say something but she cut me off.

"And don't give me one of your smart-aleck answers either."

I was like, "Mom—"

But she was on a tear. "Don't Mom me! You've got some nerve."

So I said, "Just listen, please?"

"Listen to what? Listen to you lie about what you did?"

I just shook my head.

"How can I trust you? How can I believe anything you say?"

Mom had flown past yelling and screaming and

was now into the more serious hissing-at-me-through-her-teeth stage, so I just leaned against the door and didn't say another word the whole way home.

Suffering in silence,

Dear Diary,

Things started out pretty chilly between Mom and me at breakfast this morning. I ate my cereal and read the funnies, and Mom drank coffee and did the crossword puzzle. Once in a while you'd hear my spoon clink the side of my bowl, or you'd hear Mom sip from her cup. Nothing else.

After a while we both looked up, right at the same time, and I blurted out, "I sent in the deposit before I knew we might be losing the shop."

"But Pogo—"

"I know it was wrong, Mom. But I was sure I could get the rest of the money on my own."

Mom just stared.

"I'm trying now to keep us out of collections for this. That's why I've been working so hard to make money."

Mom smiled. "Is that what you thought would happen? That the camp bill would go into collections?"

"Yeah, I thought somebody might come here looking for us."

"That's not how it works. Collections are for bills way past due. If we don't pay the rest of the money, you don't get to go to camp. Plus you might lose your deposit. That's all."

"Oh. So I don't need to worry about it?"

"I wouldn't if I were you. We've got bigger problems than that."

Just what I needed to hear.

Nervous,

Pogo

Dear Diary,

Mom's making me sleep over at Dad's tonight! Can you believe it? Making me! She never did that before. I had my night all planned out, too. I had gotten new magazines and I wanted to cut out pictures and hang them on my walls while I watch TV. But Mom said she needed some "breathing room," so she's shipping me out.

I hate when my parents boss me around.

In a bad mood,

Dear Diary,

I could have slept on the couch tonight and stayed awake really late watching TV or reading, but instead I'm in Grace's room, squeezed in on a tiny cot right next to her crib.

It's kinda weird how it happened. When I got to Dad's apartment, he was being his usual goofy self, doing dumb stuff. For one thing, right after he brought me here, he set Grace (in her baby carrier) on the table and asked me to watch her. Then he headed to his bedroom and told me he had to call Rachel, because she's away on some business trip.

I was already grouchy to the max, and that was when I finally lost it. I said, "Dad, hold it a second. I'm only staying over here 'cause I have to. I'm not your baby-sitter. As it is, I'm missing all my favorite TV shows."

So he said, "Well, go ahead and turn on the tube. Grace will probably sleep through till much later. I'll be done in just a minute anyway." Then he walked into his room and shut the door.

The click of the door closing woke Grace up. When she saw me, she smiled. I said, "Hey, you little poop, what are you smiling about, huh?"

Then, I swear on my life, the wildest thing happened—she squeezed her little fists open and closed, milkmaid style, just like Dad had showed her.

So I said, "Milk? You want milk?" And she kept doing it! I found some milk in the refrigerator. It was already in a baby bottle, so I just popped it into the microwave. I checked it on my wrist to make sure it wasn't too warm, just like I've seen on TV, then I lifted Grace out of the carrier and walked her to the couch.

I snuggled her up in the crook of my arm so she could lie down and drink. I couldn't believe her power. She started sucking like a vacuum cleaner on high, and making almost as much noise. But then, after a little while, she slowed down, nice and easy, and fell asleep in my arms.

I watched her for a few minutes, and listened to her breathe tiny little baby puffs of air. I even put my ear to her chest so I could hear her heartbeat. It fluttered so fast, tap-tap, tap-tap.

When I laid her down in her crib, I swear she smiled at me in her sleep. After that I just couldn't leave her alone so I sat next to her, rocking back and forth, in a little rocking chair.

I guess you could say, me and Grace, we bonded. Good night, *Pogo*

Dear Diary,

No wonder Dad's tired all the time. Grace wakes up the minute sunlight peeks through the curtains. She woke me up going, "Eh-eh-eh."

When I looked at the clock I said, "Shhh, Grace. Go back to sleep." But the eh-ehs got louder. I rolled over in bed and saw Grace kicking her legs up in the air. I stood up and reached into the crib. I pulled her out and noticed that she was wet and lumpy and smelling like she drank a whole lot more than milk last night.

So I said, "Let's go get Daddy up, Grace. He probably can't wait to see his big girl." Meanwhile, I'm thinking, *And I can't wait to go back to sleep.* But when Grace started to make the sign for milk, last night came rushing back and I sprang to life.

I ran to Dad's room and yelled, "Dad! Get out here! Look! Grace is doing sign language."

It took him a minute, but he finally trudged out of the room. When he saw Grace do "Milk, milk," he started laughing. He said to me, "How did you get her to do it? I've been trying to teach her that for two months! Two months." Then he took Grace from me. "Oh, Sweetums!! You precious little doll. You little cutie. Come here and give Daddy a smooch." Then he started planting little kisses all over her face.

When he finally came up for air, I said, "Shouldn't we change her diaper now?"

Dad turned to look at me, and I swear it was like he was seeing me brand new. I felt like I was a little baby again. He put his hands on my shoulders and said, "Pogo, you're amazing. My first-born daughter. My biggest girl. You're the most wonderful kid." Then tears started rolling down his cheeks like rain. And he hugged me. He just kept hugging and hugging me. Even though I was happy, I felt kind of sad, too, 'cause it reminded me of the night he left us. Just before he walked out the door, he held me for the longest while, not saying anything. And that was the only time before today that I ever saw him cry.

Finally I said, "Dad? Can you please always remember how amazing I am?" That brought on a new rush of tears, so I thought I should just stay quiet. Besides, Grace was banging on my back, wanting some attention. So I smiled at Dad and danced her into the kitchen.

Daughter Number One,

Pogo

Dear Diary,

Did you ever notice that sometimes an idea is so right-in-your-face that it hides from you? It's like one of those puzzles where you search for words. Once you find the word you're looking for, it stands out, staring at you saying, "See? I've been here the whole time. You just didn't notice me."

That's what happened today. After Iris and I helped Mr. Daly, we went to her house to fool around on the computer. We were making cards and banners and stuff. So I said, "Hey! Why don't we make up coupons for Kids' Kraft and hand them out like we did for Daly Drugs? How could we lose?"

Iris looked at the clock and said, "I want to go watch 'Zoom.' Can't we do it tomorrow?"

So I said, "Iris, 'Zoom' is a baby show. This is big stuff. If we get the flyers done now and convince my mom to let us hand them out, we could help her save the shop. Don't you want to be part of that?"

"My grandma says 'Zoom' is educational. Besides, I like it."

I gave her a look and said, "Iris, I'm not asking for so much. Please?"

Iris let out a great big sigh. Then she said, "OK, but I'm finishing quick so I can go watch. I don't care if it is a baby show." Then she turned back to the computer and started typing, humming the "Zoom" song the whole time.

Rushing,

Pogo

Later . . . That same day

Dear Diary,

In about an hour we had printed up three differ-ent kinds of coupons and flyers. Then Iris and I skated over to Kids' Kraft.

Mom was standing by one of the tables, touching up a gigantic watermelon. (Not exactly my idea of a knick-knack, if you get my drift.)

I said, "Mom, close your eyes. I have a surprise for you." She closed one but kept the other one open, scanning around the room like a scope on a subma-rine. I said, "Mom, for once in your life, be a sport." I covered her eyes.

Then Iris laid one of the coupons out on the table and said, "OK, ready."

Mom opened her eyes and read it. It said,

Make two
Make three
One of them
Is yours for free
Paint two pottery pieces
for the price of one!

When Mom saw it, she said, "What are you trying to do? Make me go broke?"

I could have said, "I thought we were broke," but I knew that wouldn't help, so I just whipped out the next coupon. It said:

Give a party
For a bunch
Ten kids or more
We provide the lunch
FREE PIZZA FOR KIDS' PARTIES

"Oh, great. First you have me giving away half the store, and now you've got me dishing out free lunches. Do you know how much a pizza costs?"

"Mom, you have to spend money to make money."

"Where'd you get that idea from? Your father?"

"Mr. Daly said it today when I asked him about discounts."

"Well, he can afford it. I can't. You know the shape we're in."

I swear, sometimes I think my mother is brain damaged. She doesn't see what's so obvious. So I motioned to Iris and she brought out the third and final item—the flyer. "What about this? We could hand these out on the sidewalk. It doesn't cost a thing." The flyer said:

PAINT A STAR
OR A CAR
SOME FLOWERS ON A JAR
PAINT THE SUN
HAVE SOME FUN
TAKE IT HOME WHEN YOU'RE DONE

KIDS' KRAFT
PAINT-IT-YOURSELF POTTERY SHOP
*PARTIES * GIFTS * CLASSES*

"Classes? Since when did I ever teach?"

"It was just an idea. You're always saying you should show people how their projects can come out more like art."

Mom rolled her eyes. "Like I have time for that."

"OK, so we'll cross that one out." I made a big X through "classes" as if to prove that I meant it. "Better?"

What could she say? No? I don't want you telling the whole world I have a store here?

She looked like she was about to turn away, but then she said, "OK. I guess it is kinda clever, this little poem you wrote."

I hugged her and said, "Now you're talking, Mom. We'll be bringing customers in here left and right, just like we did at Daly Drugs."

Then she said, "Stay close to the shop. No wandering downtown," and she went back to painting her watermelon.

I gave Iris a thumbs-up sign, and we skated out. Rolling right along,

Pogo

Dear Diary,

Iris and I printed up a whole slew of flyers. They looked great, too, 'cause Iris used her digital camera to take pictures in the store. She took a bunch near the shelves, showing all the cool things you can paint. Then she took one of me holding up a big red heart. The little hot dog and baseball boys were there, too, so Iris snapped them painting a lemon-lime ice cream soda.

Finally I put on my skates and said, "You all set, Eye?"

Iris nodded, and we zipped out.

Ready to roll,

Dear Diary,

Maybe my mom is right. Maybe sometimes I do make bad decisions. All I know is that I did a stupid thing today, and I don't know how to take it back.

Here's what happened. Iris and I skated up and down the streets near Kids' Kraft handing out the flyers. Things were going OK. We got a few parents to check out the store, and a couple of people asked us about our painting parties. But the streets by the shop were pretty quiet. That's when I got the idea to skate over to Broadway. I figured we could get more customers that way, hitting up all the commuters coming home from the train station.

Iris said, "Don't you think you should ask your mom if it's OK? I'm not supposed to go anywhere near the train tracks."

So I said, "Iris, listen. If I ask her, and she says yes, then she'll just worry till we get back and I'll never hear the end of it. If she says no, then we won't get to go. So it's better if we don't say anything. We won't cross the tracks, don't worry."

It took a little more convincing till Iris saw it my way, but we finally headed for the station, and that's when the accident happened.

We were skating down the sidewalk, with me up

ahead of Iris. I couldn't hear her skates anymore so I looked back. Iris had turned into a teeny dot in the distance. I stopped and waited for her to get close.

"Come on, Eye. You're being such a slowpoke."

"Don't 'come on' me," Iris said, huffing like a steam engine. "I'm going as fast as I can."

"But the train just came in. We have to get over there."

"Well, you get over there. It was your idea to come down here in the first place."

So I said, "Thanks a lot," and skated off. I weaved through a crowd of people—mothers pushing strollers, businessmen pushing other businessmen. Then I heard Iris scream. I looked back just in time to see her swerve around the strollers. She swerved too much, though, 'cause she skated right into the street. She disappeared between two parked cars and then I couldn't see her anymore. I sped over to the cars. Iris was lying there, her wheels caught in a sewer grate.

I said, "Thank God you didn't get hit!"

Iris started yelling. "Look what you made me do! We're not even supposed to be down here. I can't skate with all these people shoving me around."

I said, "Don't worry, Eye. I'm sure you'll be OK. Here, let me untangle your foot."

In a big whiny voice she said, "I can't even move my hand."

I didn't want her to really start crying, so I said, "Don't worry. I'm sure you'll be fine."

"This is all your fault for making me rush! I didn't even want to go skating today."

She was right. I couldn't argue about that. Plus her hand looked like it was swelling up and I was getting scared.

So I said, "I think I'd better call my mom."

Iris didn't even look at me. She just kept crying and holding her arm. Finally my mother came, and that's how I ended up here, in the emergency room, waiting and hoping and praying that Iris is all right.

In the meantime, I'm staying quiet and avoiding Mom's eyes. Every time I look up from my notebook, she's staring down at me like an owl about to swoop down on a mouse, not saying anything at all. I guess she's saving it up till we get home.

On my best behavior,

Dear Diary,

Iris sprained her wrist, which isn't terrible, but it's pretty bad. I think the damage to our friendship is worse.

When I first saw her with her hand wrapped up in an ACE bandage, I swear I felt an ache in my own wrist. I felt so bad, I almost wished I was the one who fell.

I tried to make a joke and said, "Wow, lucky you, Eye. You won't have to take any more tests this year."

But Iris said, "Yeah, and I won't be able to sign yearbooks either." Then she gave me a dirty look.

Her grandmother told her to say good-bye, and they breezed out of the hospital. I slipped into the huge revolving door in the slot right behind them and knocked on the glass, but Iris didn't turn around. I yelled, "I'll call you later," but she just kept walking, snuggled beside her grandma like a baby bird under its mother's wing.

Flying solo,

Dear Diary,

Mom's always saying I'm immature, so I figured I'd act grown up for once and admit that I did something wrong. Plus I thought admitting it might keep me from getting punished.

When we got home from the emergency room, I finally chipped through the wall of ice Mom had built up around her and said, "Mom? I want to explain to you why I skated all the way to the train station without permission."

Then I said, "I know I broke your rules, but it's because I was trying so hard to make some money for you and me."

Mom shook her head. "Make money? Look what happened to Iris. You could have gotten killed."

So I said, "I know I took a chance going down there with all that traffic. But you always have encouraged me to be a risk taker."

"Since when?"

"Since gymnastics. When I'm working on a new move and I'm scared, you always say, 'You'll never know until you try.'"

"I say that about playing the lottery, not about skating on the highway."

I wanted to say, "It's not like we were dodging cars on the New Jersey Turnpike!" But I just said,

"I'm sorry. I made a bad decision."

Mom squinted her eyes and flared her nostrils, a face that always puts me on the verge of hysterical laughter. I guess a smile leaked out, 'cause Mom said, "What's so funny?"

I couldn't help it. I said, "Mom, you look like a bull about to charge."

That finally got her to ease up a little. She came over to me and said, "I couldn't bear it if I lost you."

I thought maybe Mom was going overboard, but I nodded anyway.

"Don't you realize what could have happened to you and Iris?"

I nodded again.

"You really scared me, Pogo."

If I nodded any more, I'd turn into one of those freaky toy dogs people keep in their car windows, so I said, "Mom, I'm right here." Then I hugged her.

She didn't say anything about a punishment, so I didn't make any suggestions.

Back on Mom's good side,

Thursday, June 13

Dear Diary,

Iris didn't come to school today. I tried to call her, but her grandmother said Iris needs her rest. Is she really resting, or does she just not want to talk to me?

On Iris's bad side,

Saturday, June 15 . . . After breakfast

Dear Diary,

I spent the night at Dad's, and this morning he asked me to help him make breakfast. I don't know where he got the idea that I could cook. He should know I take after Mom in that department. Plus I couldn't really concentrate because things are so messed up with Iris.

I had this urge to call her. I even went to the phone and started dialing. It was kind of automatic. If I could at least talk to her, things would feel a little better. But then I remembered her face, all hard and shut tight against me, and I lost power in my dialing finger.

I wasn't paying attention to anything else and I almost stepped on Grace, who was sitting on the kitchen floor. She was busy eating her sock. I took it out of her mouth and said, "No, no, Grace. Don't eat that."

Dad said to me, "Look. Give her the sign for 'no.'" Then he made the duck-quacking sign.

After I told Grace "no" she poked me and made a sign with her two hands like claws, one stretching above the other.

So I said, "Dad! This kid is talking up a storm, but I have no idea what she wants."

Dad squatted down and said, "She's saying 'cake.'

I guess she wants cake. Is that it, Gracie? Well, Daddy has to make a cake. You want to make cake?" Then he picked her up and started singing, "Pat-a-cake, pat-a-cake, baker's man . . ."

Grace patted Dad on the forehead.

". . . Bake me a cake as fast as you can."

I said, "Dad? I hate to interrupt, but the eggs aren't looking very sunny anymore."

But Dad just took Grace's hand and rolled it and rolled it and marked it with a B, so I knew I would have to wait till the song ended.

"Put it in the oven . . ."

Then it hit me: cake. Iris's favorite snack. That would soften her up.

So I rummaged around in the cabinets till I found not one but two cake mixes. I put the boxes on the counter and said, "Here we go, Dad. One for your family and one for mine."

Just call me
      Betty *Pogo* Crocker

Dear Diary,

When I finished decorating Iris's cake with a great big eyeball (for Iris, get it?), I felt so happy and proud, I danced around Dad's kitchen. I pulled Grace out of her high chair and took her for a spin. As soon as I turned on the disco music, Grace wiggled her fingers over her palms, making a sign. At first I thought maybe she wanted me to put her down, but she was laughing and drooling like a puppy so I knew she liked the ride.

Then it dawned on me! "Dance! You're saying 'dance'! Your two little fingers are legs, right?" Dad confirmed it for me. "I guess this sign-language stuff isn't so hard after all, is it Grace?"

Then I thought, *Now if I can just figure out how to talk to Iris, I'll be all set.*

Hoping my cake does the trick, Pogo

Dear Diary,

When Dad dropped me off at Iris's house, she answered the door, but she didn't step outside. I didn't want to say anything goofy, so I just presented her with the cake like I was offering her a prize. Iris looked down at it and said, "My eyes are blue, in case you haven't noticed."

"I only had brown icing, Eye."

"What's the occasion?"

"I wanted to say I'm sorry."

"You should be. You made me go sprawling all over Broadway in my Rollerblades."

"I know. I really messed up."

"That's for sure." Then she grabbed the cake with one hand and shut the door with her foot.

I stood there for a second with the door closed in my face and thought, *Why didn't she use some of that coordination when she was skating?*

Still out in the cold,

Monday, June 17 . . . Afternoon

Dear Diary,
Iris is back in school but she ignored me all day.
Sad,

Dear Diary,

Usually the last week of school is such a blast. We play outdoor games and eat picnic lunches. The teachers are all smiley, and nobody ever gets in trouble.

Today I was hyper and happied up 'cause we were having track-and-field day (my favorite), then free time.

But right from the start, things went wrong. I fell in the sand when I did my standing long jump, and that's usually my best event. Then my team lost both of our relay races. After that I couldn't find my lunch so I had to eat baloney from school and I hate baloney.

But the worst happened after lunch.

Some of the girls from the gymnastics team were goofing around, playing Copycat-and-a-Half, which starts when one girl does a trick, and then the next girl has to do the same trick and add her own. It keeps going like that until somebody forgets a move—then she's out. It gets very silly.

I was playing and I saw Iris videotaping off to the side. So I called out to her, "Hey, Iris. Why don't you tape our game?"

She put her eye up above the camera lens. Then, I swear, she made the meanest face. I didn't even know Iris could give such a dirty look. Then she shut the camera off and turned around.

All the other girls were staring at me like, "What are you gonna do now?" So I just laughed and acted like Iris was making a joke. But deep down inside I felt like somebody had stuck me with a needle and drained out all my blood.

Wouldn't you know, it was my turn for Copycat and I couldn't remember any of the tricks.

Of course, Victoria piped up and said, "What's the matter? Can't you do my move?"

I wanted to punch her. I wanted to flatten her right out. But before I could even say one word, Victoria finished me off. "Well, I can always teach you when we're at camp. That is . . . if you're still going."

Crushed,

Dear Diary,

Did you ever walk into your house and know just by the smell that something was wrong? It's almost like the house says, "Whoa, wait a second. Are you sure you want to come in?" You sense this unspoken warning that tells you something big and powerful is happening inside these four walls and you might want to back off.

If that never happened to you, count yourself lucky. 'Cause that happened to me today when I came home from the last day of school. I walked up to the house and I felt that smell. I didn't even *smell* it—I *felt* it.

This was big.

Sure enough, I walked into the kitchen at 3:30 in the afternoon and there sat Mom, in her bathrobe, smoking a cigarette. And she doesn't even smoke.

So I said, "Mom, what's wrong? Aren't we going back to the shop?"

She takes this really big puff off the cigarette and lets it out real slow. I swear I thought I was in a movie. Then she says to me, "I closed it."

Naturally I said, "Why? What happened?"

So she said, "The power company threatened to turn off the electricity, so I turned it off myself. No point in running a shop in the dark, is there?"

I said, "But they're just threatening us, right?" I knew that they would only keep us lit if Mom sent in some money.

So Mom said, "What's the point? Today it's the power. Tomorrow it will be the water. I give up. I can't run it anymore."

The scary thing was, she didn't even cry. She just looked numb and white.

I wanted to say something, but every time I opened my mouth, it felt all gluey and stuck together. Then my throat closed up and I choked back sharp, jagged tears. I felt like a baby, and I wondered if this is how Grace feels all the time, wanting so badly to talk but having no words.

I sat down next to Mom (even though I detest the smell of smoke) and I put my head on her chest. When Mom put her arm around me and started stroking my hair, I felt tears running down her face and dripping onto my forehead.

I never knew tears could feel so cold.

Wishing for words,

That evening

Dear Diary,

This is the first time in five years that I've hated the last day of school. Why? Because Iris and I have a ritual, and this year we didn't follow it.

Usually she stays over at my house, and we stay up as late as we can, eating pizza and watching movies. Then we sleep late the next day. After we eat a huge breakfast, we make a list of all the cool things we're going to do for the next two months.

But not this year.

So far my list has only two items on it:

1. Clean out Kids' Kraft and close up the shop.

2. Make up with Iris.

Some summer vacation.

Lights out,

Thursday, June 20 . . . 7:00 A.M.

Dear Diary,

I never expected Mom to be up so early this morning. I thought, for sure, this would be one of her stay-in-bed-reading days. But no. I was finishing my last dream when she charged into my room, slapping open the shades and calling my name.

I slammed my eyelids shut, hoping she'd leave me alone. Instead, she sat down on my bed and started telling me about our plans for the day—the plan for shutting down Kids' Kraft. She rattled on and on about how maybe we could have a tag sale to get rid of some of the stuff from the shop. Or how we could donate some of the pieces to an old folks' home or a hospital.

When she finally came up for a breath of air, I broke in and said, "Have you been up all night drinking coffee again?"

Mom stared at me. "I couldn't sleep."

"So that's it? The shop is over and we have no way to get money now?"

"I saved us a last little bit for emergencies. At least we won't starve."

I sat up. "You're letting go? Just like that? You're not even going to try?"

"What do you want me to do? I'm already going gray worrying about the place."

"But you're the one who always tells me not to give up."

Mom took my hand. "Listen. It's not like I'm giving up on life. I'm just facing reality. And I definitely think it's time to move on. For both of us."

"Move on to what?"

Mom didn't have an answer to that. She just sat on my bed for the longest time, probably expecting me to get up, but when she saw I wouldn't budge, she left my room.

Not moving anywhere, *Pogo*

Dear Diary,

I don't know why grown-ups are so big on this idea of facing reality. The counselor at school is, too. A few weeks after my dad moved out, he made this plan to come back and get his stuff. My parents asked me if I wanted to stay around for that and help him decide what to take. I was like, "Hello, I don't think I want to be around when half my family leaves." But my counselor said maybe I should try. She told me it would help me to accept the divorce if I took part in the process. She told me not to run away from it.

I guess that's what Mom is talking about, too, when she says I have to face reality and move on. But what she doesn't get is this: When my dad was leaving, I knew he was just moving across town. I knew I could see him whenever I wanted to.

This is different. Mom's moving on and she's taking me with her. But who knows where?

Feeling lost,

Friday, June 21 . . . In the car

Dear Diary,

I got out of cleaning up Kids' Kraft yesterday but not today. Mom had to drag me out of my room when it was time to go. She keeps throwing me looks, but I just pretend I'm writing in here. I don't feel like talking, I don't feel like listening, and I especially don't feel like cleaning up.

In my own world,

Dear Diary,

Mom said it was my job to sort through the left-over pottery pieces in the back room and make two piles—"save" and "junk." I never knew it would be so hard to throw away old stuff. I used to love cleaning up and getting rid of things. But now it feels so . . . forever.

I was rummaging through a big box when I found the baseball and hot dog the two little boys painted with me that day. The pieces were finished, but I guess the kids must have left them to dry, then never came back to pick them up. I put those in the save pile, just in case.

I was about to abandon the box and take a writing break when I saw the rim of a flowerpot sticking out. Instantly, I remembered the day Iris and I painted it. We had this idea last summer to grow plants. In school we had a garden project going on. Our teacher got us to cut up milk cartons and use them as planters. We grew beans and flowers. We experimented with different amounts of sunlight and water. Every day we raced into the classroom to see if our plants had changed overnight. By the time school let out, Iris and I were ready to start our own garden.

Looking at the unfinished flowerpot, I wondered

why we ever stopped working on it. Half a sun-flower was painted on the front, and the beginning of a leafy border trailed around the edge. I knew I couldn't throw the pot away, but the emptiness of it got to me. I felt like I had to fill it and grow some-thing big and beautiful inside. And I knew I didn't want to grow it by myself.

Missing Iris,

Dear Diary,

I walked slowly, planning out what I would say to Iris. If I could make her laugh or at least just get her to smile, maybe things would be OK. Things had to be OK between us, 'cause nothing else in my life was.

Iris was outside taking pictures when I walked up to her house. I held my breath while she focused in on a butterfly landing on a leaf. She snapped the photo, then turned to look at me.

I forced a smile and held up the flowerpot. "It needs a little something, don't you think?"

Iris didn't smile. "What? You probably want my help again, right?"

I felt like she shot me with a dart. "Are you going to be mad at me forever, Iris?"

"Oh, so you can be mad at me, but I can't get mad back?"

"I don't understand you. I said I was sorry."

"I'm just sticking up for myself like you told me to, Pogo. Only now you don't like it."

"What do you mean, sticking up for yourself?"

"You told me kids pick on me 'cause I don't fight back. You told me to tell somebody off once in a while. So now I am." Iris's voice shook, but she kept on. "You did a mean thing, Pogo, convincing me to do something I didn't want to do."

"I already apologized for it."

"It's not just that. I'm tired of you bossing me around. We never do what I want to do. We never play dolls anymore. And you always say my ideas are goofy."

"Iris—"

She put her hand up to stop me. "And now you're probably here 'cause you want me to help you plant flowers and sell them, right?"

So I said, "No, Iris. Wrong answer." And before I could hold myself back, I started sobbing like Grace would, and my story spilled out like milk on the lunchroom floor.

I told Iris about the store closing and how my mom had no more money. I told her it felt like my life was falling apart.

Iris just listened for a long time and said "uh-uh" in all the right places. Which is really what you want a friend to do. She even got me some Burger King napkins from her grandma's car so I could wipe my face and blow my nose.

When I finished telling her my problems I said, "I'm sorry I'm such a bad friend to you, Iris. I never meant to be selfish." Then I picked up the flowerpot and said, "Will you finish this with me? Just for fun?"

She nodded and smiled. I cried some happy tears then 'cause I knew the old Iris was back.

Feeling a little better,

Pogo

Dear Diary,

Mom let me bring Iris to the store today. I convinced Mom we could get more done with some extra help. When we went to pick up Iris, though, what should I see in her yard but the big Clifford dog that almost ruined my gymnastics show. I was already on my way to the front door when he bounded up and stopped to sniff me. I just stood, frozen like an ice cube in Alaska, praying he wouldn't sink his teeth into my bare leg. But then he licked me!!! He licked my hand with his big, sloppy tongue. I was so happy he wasn't attacking me, I rubbed his head and said, "Nice boy. Good doggie." I was still shaking a little bit, but at least I could move my body parts.

When Iris finally came outside, I was petting the dog and really making friends with him. I said to Iris, "Do you think I could learn to like dogs and not be afraid of them?"

"Yeah, sure. Why not?"

"I think I might try that."

"I can show you how to get friendly with any animal. All you have to do is give it treats."

"That's all there is to it? I could do that. And then we could make pet videos like you wanted."

Iris's face lit up. "That would be great. And

speaking of videos, I made another one I want to show you. You'll love this one."

Iris and I babbled on and on about animals and a million other things for the rest of the ride. We hardly noticed when Mom pulled up in front of the shop.

On my way to a good summer, *Pogo*

Dear Diary,

Iris brought her camera, and right away she started snapping pictures in the back of the store. She said we needed to save all our memories of Kids' Kraft. I thought she was crazy, 'cause the shelves were half-empty and the back room was almost bare, except for the bags and boxes of junk. Leave it to Iris to find something really cool in all that. I watched for a few minutes while she arranged some old pieces, one by one, in a row, then built a pyramid.

Finally I got to sorting again. I thought to myself, *If Mom has any hopes of selling this stuff or even giving it away, she might have to make other plans.*

"Hey, Eye! Look at this! You think they left it on purpose?" I held up a hamburger painted red, white, and blue. "Like you'd really display that, huh?"

Then I picked up a plate designed like a happy face with words written in place of the smile. I squinted to read it. "It says 'It's nice to be nice.'" Then I looked again. "Or does it say 'It's nice to be rice.' The paint is so smudged, I can't tell."

I put those two things in the junk pile and looked for more.

Just then the swinging door pushed open a little way, and Grace came crawling in on all fours.

"Gracie Baby! What are you doing here?" I ran

over and scooped her up.

"Iris! Take some pictures of my little sister. Look at her face. Isn't she cute?"

Iris started snapping away. Of course, she wanted unusual pictures, like one of the bottom of Grace's feet and one of her tiny nails. I think she even took a picture of the inside of Grace's ear.

"Watch this, Iris!" I held Grace out in front of me. "Grace, you want to do a flip?" She giggled. I gently flipped her backward through my arms.

"Come on, Grace! Let's spin." I swung Grace in circles, lifting her high, then swinging her low.

Then I put Grace down on the floor and sat next to her. "OK, now. Show Iris how you roll."

Grace just sat.

"Come on! You can do it." I made my hands into fists and pumped them around in a circle. Grace didn't move. Then I did a forward roll myself.

Finally Grace understood. She rolled onto her side, then onto her back. Just as she did that, Iris snapped another photo—and that's when I got my biggest flash of inspiration.

I grabbed Grace and kissed her. "I've got it! Grace! You just gave me an idea! Oh, you beautiful baby! Iris! Listen to this and tell me what you think!"

Bubbling over, *Pogo*

Dear Diary,

At first, I didn't want to write about my idea in here because I thought I might jinx it. But now I have to, because I'm ready to pop!

It's a playroom and mini-gym for little kids!! Great, right?

That's if Mom goes for it. I first told her about the idea yesterday, but all she said was, "Oh, I'll think about it." And went right ahead throwing stuff out.

The last time I brought up the idea, which was about five minutes ago, Mom just gave me the evil eye, and I knew that meant, "Stop pestering me and get back to cleaning."

But I can't concentrate. Every little thing makes me jump. Waiting for Mom to make a decision is like waiting to get a test back. You're dying to know if you passed or failed, but at the same time you're scared to find out.

Hanging by a thread,

Dear Diary,

Things are not looking good. This morning when I went downstairs for breakfast, I found Mom sitting at the counter, circling job ads for a secretary.

I said, "You? A secretary?"

And Mom said, "Well, I have to do something."

"I thought you said you didn't even believe in having a boss."

"Well, I believe in having a paycheck. I know that."

I didn't want to be mean, but I had to change Mom's mind and get her off this track.

"Mom, you can't even type."

She flung the paper across the table. "Well, you're a big help this morning! What do you want me to do?"

"I thought maybe you were working on my idea."

Mom didn't say anything.

"So you're not?"

"I didn't say that."

"You aren't. If you were, you would have said so. Don't you think it's a good idea?"

"I do. I think it's really good. But things like that take time. Can't you just let it go for a while?"

"We don't have a while."

"I'm doing . . . what . . . I can. Now leave it alone."

I knew by Mom's tone that I was at my limit of bugging, asking, and whining, so I left the room. But this isn't the end of it.

Not letting go of anything,

Dear Diary,

I don't know if things could get any worse. Mom got rid of the tables in the shop. And just a little while ago, somebody barged in here and put up a sign in the front window that said "For Rent." After he left, and Mom wasn't looking, I turned the sign around and drew a mad face on the back of it.

Then I walked into Mom's office, where she was organizing her papers and getting rid of the last of her stuff.

I said, "Mom, are we already kicked out of here?"

She said, "We didn't get kicked out. We decided to leave. And we have two more days to go."

I took a deep breath. "So then are you still thinking about my idea?"

"Pogo, please? I've got a million other things to think about right now."

"But Mom, you say that every time I ask."

"Well, then stop asking!"

"Then you'll never think about it."

"I will. I promise. I'm just too busy right now."

"So much for you listening to me!" I stormed out of her office into the front room. I kicked the disco ball that was sitting by itself in the empty shop. One of the little mirrored tiles fell off, and I felt bad. When I first found the ball hidden away in a closet of the shop, I loved it. I loved twirling it and watching the light flashes that sprayed on the wall. Mom let me save it even though she said, "What do you want that for? It's missing half the tiles."

I said, "So what? It's still beautiful. I'll fix it and hang it from the ceiling by my glow-in-the-dark stars."

But now when I held it, nothing glittered because outside the sky was dark and cloudy. And when I looked at the bald spots where the mirrors had dropped off, I saw what Mom saw: a broken, used-to-be thing. When I peered into it to try to see my reflection, my face looked broken, too.

Holding it all in,

Pogo

Dear Diary,

Just like I stormed out of Mom's office, I stormed back in and said, "What are you going to do? Ignore me and hope I go away?"

"What are you talking about?"

"Just like you do with everything else in your life?"

"What?"

"Like you did with camp, and I had to send in my own money?"

"Pogo—"

"Like you did with you and Daddy?"

Uh-oh. I don't know why I said that last one. That was definitely not part of the plan. I think I stopped breathing for about five minutes while I waited for Mom's reaction.

But the weird thing was, it never came. No hot lava shooting out of the volcano. No dynamite exploding. Mom didn't say a thing. She just stared. Then she licked an envelope, sealed it, and laid it on her desk.

Scared to know what she's thinking,

Dear Diary,

Mom kinda gave me the silent treatment today after I got mad at her. But when we got home, she said, "Come here. I want to show you something."

The way she said it, so serious and hard, I felt as if it was going to be like one of those moments when parents sit you down and tell you the facts of life. Or like when somebody tells you your cat died.

Mom took a packet of papers out of her safety box. She unfolded it slowly and carefully on the table, like it was a letter from the president.

"This is a business proposal. Do you know what that means?"

"Sort of."

"It's my plan to start a new company. Our new company. Your idea. I gave it to the bank and I'm waiting for a loan to be approved."

It took a few seconds for that to sink in.

"I didn't want to tell you because I didn't want you to get your hopes up."

I still didn't say anything.

Mom put her hands on my shoulders. "Dirt to Pogo. Come in, Pogo. Blink once if you follow what I'm saying."

"I hear you, Mom."

"Well, isn't this what you wanted?"

"It is. I just don't get why you didn't tell me sooner."

"I didn't want you to be disappointed if the bank turns us down."

"When are we supposed to find out?"

"Any day now. Mr. George said they could rush it because they know me. But the only way he'd even look at the proposal was if I put the last of my emergency savings toward the bill. So please, don't start making any big plans. There's only a slim chance that they'll lend us any money."

I said yes to Mom at the moment, but in my head the wheels started turning, and they've been turning ever since.

Not good at waiting,

Dear Diary,

Here's my plan:

1. Give Mom the rest of the camp money to help pay the bills.

2. Go to the bank with Iris at 9:00 A.M.

3. Spy. Figure out who Mr. George is. (I think he's the bald-headed guy with the big desk, who always flirts with Mom when we go in to get change for the shop.)

4. Talk to him and convince him how much we need a kids' playroom in our town.

5. Hint to Mr. George that Mom likes him?

Scheming,

Dear Diary,

So much for going to the bank and sweet-talking Mr. George. Mom forced me to come to the shop with her today. I tried to tell her it would be too painful watching while strangers walked through talking about turning it into a dry cleaner or a fabric store. But Mom didn't go for it. She got me here and steered me to the back room and pointed to the save and junk piles. Then she said, "See if you can be a little more discerning."

I must have looked confused 'cause Mom said, "Save a few really important things and throw out the rest."

I just stood there, wondering how I was going to get to the bank. I think Mom mistook that look for sadness, 'cause she got all teary-eyed and sat me down. Then she said, "Do you know why it's so important to say good-bye?"

I thought maybe it was a trick question, so I didn't say anything.

Of course, Mom had an answer all ready and waiting. "If you say good-bye, Pogo, it makes it easier to say hello again."

And then she walked out, like she had just solved the world's problems with that one little comment.

Not saying hello or good-bye, *Pogo*

Friday, June 28 . . . 3:00 P.M.

Dear Diary,

Just when I thought I would burst from not knowing, the bank called and said we got the loan! The bank said yes! Yes, yes, yes!

More later! I have to run and tell Iris!

Bouncing off the walls,

Dear Diary,

This is the latest: Mom's letting me name the gym! I guess that's my reward for coming up with such a great idea!

Just call me,

Pogo of "Pogo's Playroom"

Dear Diary,

Mom almost didn't let me go shopping with her when she went to look at equipment for the Playroom. But I said, "Mom, duh. It's stuff for kids. How will you know if it's fun unless I try it out?" She finally said OK and I even convinced her to let me bring Iris.

I could tell that Mom was really nervous when she looked at the equipment. Even though she had money from the bank, she still got a heart attack every time she saw the price of anything.

But I had a blast. We shopped all afternoon. First we looked at one of those long tubes to wiggle through. The only bad part was Iris just had to try it out after she saw me do it. I warned her. I said, "Iris, it's really for little kids. Maybe you'd better not." But she squeezed in anyway. Then Mom and I had to yank her out 'cause she got stuck halfway through. Mom bought the tube, though, and said we'll just have to keep a close eye on anybody who uses it.

Next Mom asked us to go try out a jungle gym. I think Iris was a little nervous—she just watched this time. I couldn't really swing from the bars 'cause they hang too low, but we bought it, anyway. We knew smaller kids would love it.

We saved the best for last: the Air Jump. It's a big inflatable bubble to bounce in. We even convinced Mom to get in and fool around with us. We all kicked off our sneakers and jumped inside for a long time. Iris says she likes the Air Jump even better than the trampoline, 'cause you can flop around in it without worrying how you land. Believe me, if they ever had a contest for flopping, Iris would definitely win.

Shopping and flopping,

Pogo

Dear Diary,

You are not going to believe what happened today! I invited all the girls from the gymnastics team to the Playroom, even Icky Vicky. Most of the equipment is in, and I thought it would be fun to show it off. I may not be going to gymnastics camp, but I want everybody, especially Victoria, to know I'll be having a great summer.

We all played for a while on the stuff, even though a lot of it is for little kids. The floor is covered with mats in funky orange, yellow, and red—so it's like heaven for us—you can do gymnastics anywhere. We chased each other across the flying bridge, which is this long stretch of rubber that swings when you walk on it. It leads to a spaceship, which you can "drive." That's all up above. So is the tree house, which you enter through a secret passageway. Kids are gonna love this place!!!

That stuff is all in the front room. So is the sandbox, the hideaway cave, and the costumes for dress-up.

When we got tired of the little-kid things, we went into the back. That's where we'll be having all our groups—classes for babies and moms or dads, and classes for toddlers and four- and five-year-olds. The back room is covered wall-to-wall in mats, with a few pieces of equipment.

When Victoria got on the low beam to show off, everybody watched. (She's the best on the beam. Of course, she takes private lessons with a coach, so why shouldn't she be?) When she finished her routine, I gave Iris "the sign" and called to the girls.

"Hey, everybody! Iris has a video she wants to show. Come on and watch. All of you are in it."

Iris popped the tape into our new VCR.

When Victoria saw herself on the screen, she said, "Shhh, shhh, quiet everybody, watch!"

Little did Miss Perfect know that Iris had caught her in some not-so-private moments. The first one was of her yanking at her leotard. It happens to all of us—the thing slides up your rear and you pull it back down as quickly as you can. I guess it was just the look on Victoria's face and the way she struggled when she did it that made everybody giggle. And she kept doing it!

Then, I don't know how Iris captured this one, but she got a very long shot of Victoria picking her nose, then trying to get rid of it! Everybody was like, "eeeeewwwwww."

I couldn't believe it. I told Iris to stand up to people with her words, but I guess it's true—a picture's worth a thousand of them! Icky Vicky was not a very good sport. She stood up and gave me and

Iris a burning glare. Then she stormed out of the room. Steam was coming out of her ears, I swear!

Still laughing,

Pogo

Dear Diary,

I invited Grace to our new place today. I wanted to give her a chance to have some fun in here before we open for business tomorrow and I don't have time. Didn't I tell you? I'm the assistant gymnastics coach! Mom hired a teacher for our weekend tot parties and I'm her helper. So even though Grace will be here celebrating with us, I won't be able to play with her much.

When Dad brought Grace in, he handed her to me, and then he actually stayed and had a conversation with Mom.

I put Grace on the floor and let her crawl around on the mats. I can't believe how fast she scrambled across the floor. I swear I blinked my eyes and she was over at the slide, pointing up.

"Hey, Gracie. You want to get on there?" (Even I could figure out that's what she meant.)

I held her and we climbed up the four little steps. Then I sat her on my lap and we slid down. It was really a very short ride, but Grace laughed the whole way. Then she made me bring her up about five hundred more times. (If there's a baby sign for the word "again," she definitely would have worn it out today.)

Finally I put Grace down and laid beside her on

the mats. I told her, "No more, Grace. I'm pooped."

Then she did the cutest thing. She crawled right over to my side and butted her head against me like a dog would, like she wanted to be petted.

I started rubbing her on the head, and I felt this little soft spot. It was right on the top, where her hair is silky and fine like down feathers. I was rubbing and thinking about that spot, how it wasn't hard like the rest of her head. I was thinking that maybe she wasn't all formed yet, or maybe she was born with something missing. I got a little scared, but then I thought, maybe that's just the way babies are. Maybe it's a good thing she's not totally hard in the head. I started to wonder if maybe that baby softness lets things pass through more easily than when you're a grown-up kid. I mean like love and good stuff. 'Cause Grace just loves everybody and everything, and she laughs for no reason. And even if she falls, she just gets back up and starts all over again.

I leaned down and kissed her on that soft spot, and she just laughed like it tickled. Then I lifted her up and put my feet on her stomach. "Wanna go for a ride, Gracie Grace?" I bet she knows about the airplane, 'cause Dad used to fly me all the time. Even when I got big he played airplane with me.

Grace loved it. She made the little "Eeeeeeeee"

sound every time I zipped her back and forth. "Just wait, little girl. I'll get you doing gymnastics before you learn to walk."

Flying high, *Pogo*

Dear Diary,

Finally! The big day is here. I'm just waiting for Iris. She has her own job in the Playroom, taking pictures of the party kids and selling them to the families.

Dad's already here, and it's totally OK. He actually brought Mom flowers and wished her good luck. Then he told her he wouldn't have missed her opening for the world.

It's a good thing I'm all ready 'cause the phone is ringing off the hook, and I'm supposed to answer it. People are calling non-stop to sign up for Tumblin' Tot parties. We've already booked six for this month and two for August.

Bouncing back,

Dear Diary,

Yup, you read that right. I'm at camp. I got here early and claimed the top bunk.

To tell you the truth, I got so involved with the Playroom, I was almost too busy to think about camp. It hit me right after I scheduled a party for July 22. That was when I grabbed Mom and showed her the little "C.S." I had written on the calendar. I said to her, "What do you think? Can I go?"

I was a little surprised when Mom told me she'd already sent in the money. But she just winked and said, "Are you kidding? Did you really think I wouldn't let you go? And waste all that potential?"

Flying High,
Pogo!

Meet the Author

Constance M. Foland

Then

Now

Growing up, Constance Foland loved gymnastics. She created her own routines and liked to show off in front of friends. Today she lives in New York City, where she teaches elementary school. Constance writes in a journal every day and carries it with her wherever she goes.